Goosebumps

Attack of the Mutant

"I have to go back," I said, turning to leave.

And as I turned, something came into view that made my breath catch in my throat.

"Ohh." I let out a startled cry and stared across the street. "But—that's *impossible*!" I exclaimed.

I was staring at a tall building on the other corner. A tall, pink stucco building with a bright green, domed roof.

I was staring at the secret headquarters of The Masked Mutant.

Goosebumps

Attack of the Mutant

R.L. Stine

Scholastic Children's Books,
Commonwealth House, 1–19 New Oxford Street,
London WC1A 1NU
a division of Scholastic Ltd
London ~ New York ~ Toronto ~ Sydney ~ Auckland

First published in the USA by Scholastic Inc., 1994
First published in the UK by Scholastic Ltd, 1995

ISBN 0 590 13240 7

Typeset by Contour Typesetters, Southall, London
Printed by Cox & Wyman Ltd, Reading, Berks

10 9 8 7 6 5 4 3 2 1

"Hey—put that down!"

I grabbed the comic book from Wilson Clark's hand and smoothed out the plastic cover.

"I was only looking at it," he grumbled.

"If you get a fingerprint on it, it will lose half its value," I told him. I examined the cover through the clear wrapper. "This is a *Silver Swan* Number Zero," I said. "And it's in mint condition."

Wilson shook his head. He has curly, white-blond hair and round, blue eyes. He always looks confused.

"How can it be Number Zero?" he asked. "That doesn't make any sense, Skipper."

Wilson is a really good friend of mine. But sometimes I think he dropped down from the planet Mars. He just doesn't know *anything*.

I held up the *Silver Swan* cover so he could see the big zero in the corner. "That makes it a collector's item," I explained. "Number Zero

1

comes before Number One. This comic is worth ten times as much as *Silver Swan* Number One."

"Huh? It is?" Wilson scratched his curly hair. He squatted down on the floor and started pawing through my box of comic books. "How come all your comics are in these plastic bags, Skipper? How can you read them?"

See? I told you. Wilson doesn't know anything.

"Read them? I don't read them," I replied. "If you read them, they lose their value."

He stared up at me. "You don't read them?"

"I can't take them out of the bag," I explained. "If I open the bag, they won't be in mint condition any more."

"Ooh. This one is cool!" he exclaimed. He pulled up a copy of *Star Wolf.* "The cover is metal!"

"It's worthless," I mumbled. "It's a second printing."

He stared at the silvery cover, turning it in his hands, making it shine in the light. "Cool," he muttered. His favourite word.

We were up in my room, about an hour after dinner. The sky was black outside my double windows. It gets dark so early in winter. Not like on the Silver Swan's planet, Orcos III, where the sun never sets and all the superheroes have to wear air-conditioned costumes.

Wilson had come over to get the maths homework. He lives next door, and he always leaves

2

his maths book at school—so he always comes over to get the homework from me.

"You should collect comic books," I told him. "In about twenty years, these will be worth millions."

"I collect rubber stamps," he said, picking up a *Z-Squad* annual. He studied the trainer ad on the back cover.

"Rubber stamps?"

"Yeah. I have about a hundred of them," he said.

"What can you do with rubber stamps?" I asked.

He dropped the comic back into the box and stood up. "Well, you can stamp things with them," he said, brushing off the knees of his jeans. "I have different-coloured ink pads. Or you can just look at them."

He is definitely weird.

"Are they valuable?" I asked.

He shook his head. "I don't think so." He picked up the maths sheet from the foot of my bed. "I'd better get home, Skipper. See you tomorrow."

He started for the door and I followed him. Our reflections stared out at us from my big dressing-table mirror. Wilson is so tall and skinny and blond and blue-eyed. I always feel like a dark, chubby mole next to him.

If we were in a comic book, Wilson would be

3

the superhero, and I would be his sidekick. I'd be the pudgy, funny one who was always messing up.

It's a good thing life isn't a comic book—right?

As soon as Wilson left, I turned back to my dressing-table. My eye caught the big computer banner above the mirror: SKIPPER MATTHEWS, ALIEN AVENGER.

My dad had got someone at his office to print out the banner for me for my twelfth birthday a few weeks ago.

Beneath the banner, I have two great posters tacked on the wall on both sides of the dressing-table. One is a Jack Kirby *Captain America*. It's really old and probably worth about a thousand dollars.

The other one is newer—a *Spawn* poster by Todd McFarlane. It's really awesome.

In the mirror, I could see the excited look on my own face as I hurried to the dressing-table.

The flat brown envelope waited for me on the dressing-table.

Mum and Dad said I couldn't open it until after dinner, after I finished my homework. But I couldn't wait.

I could feel my heart start to pound as I stared down at the envelope.

I knew what waited inside it. Just thinking about it made my heart pound even harder.

I carefully picked up the envelope. I had to open it now. I *had* to.

Carefully, carefully, I tore the flap on the envelope. Then I reached inside and pulled out the treasure.

This month's issue of *The Masked Mutant*.

Holding the comic book in both hands, I studied the cover. *The Masked Mutant 24*. In jagged red letters across the bottom, I read:

"A TIGHT SQUEEZE
FOR THE SENSATIONAL SPONGE!"

The cover art was awesome. It showed SpongeLife—known across the universe as The Sponge of Steel—in terrible trouble. He was caught in the tentacles of a gigantic octopus. The octopus was squeezing him dry!

Awesome. Totally awesome.

I keep all of my comic books in mint condition, wrapped in collector's bags. But there is one comic that I have to read every month. And that's *The Masked Mutant*.

I have to read it as soon as it comes out. And I

read it cover to cover, every word in every panel. I even read the Letters page.

That's because *The Masked Mutant* is the best-drawn, best-written comic in the world. And The Masked Mutant *has* to be the most powerful, most evil villain ever created!

What makes him so terrifying is that he can move his molecules around.

That means he can change himself into anything that's solid. *Anything!*

On this cover, the giant octopus is actually The Masked Mutant. You can tell because the octopus is wearing the mask that The Masked Mutant always wears.

But he can change himself into *any* animal. Or any object.

That's how he always escapes from The League of Good Guys. There are six different superheroes in The League of Good Guys. They are all mutants, too, with amazing powers. And they are the world's best law enforcers. But they can't catch The Masked Mutant.

Even the League's leader—The Galloping Gazelle—the fastest man in the solar system, isn't fast enough to keep up with The Masked Mutant.

I studied the cover for a few minutes. I liked the way the octopus tentacles squeezed Sponge-Life into a limp rag. You could see by his expression that The Sponge of Steel was in mortal pain.

Awesome.

I carried the comic over to the bed and sprawled on to my stomach to read it. The story began where *The Masked Mutant 23* left off.

SpongeLife, the world's best underwater swimmer, was deep in the ocean. He was desperately trying to escape from The Masked Mutant. But The Sponge of Steel had caught his cape on the edge of a coral reef.

I turned the page. As The Masked Mutant drew nearer, he began to move his molecules around. And he changed himself into a huge, really gross octopus.

There were eight drawings showing The Masked Mutant transform himself. And then came a big, full-page drawing showing the enormous octopus reaching out its slimy, fat tentacles to grab the helpless SpongeLife.

SpongeLife struggled to pull away.

But the octopus tentacles slid closer. Closer.

I started to turn the page. But before I could move, I felt something cold and slimy wrap itself around *my* neck.

I let out a gasp and tried to struggle free.

But the cold tentacles wrapped themselves tighter around my throat.

I couldn't move. I couldn't scream.

I heard laughter.

With a great effort, I turned around. And saw Mitzi, my nine-year-old sister. She pulled her hands away from my neck and jumped back as I glared at her.

"Why are your hands so cold?" I demanded.

She smiled at me with her innocent, two-dimpled smile. "I put them in the refrigerator."

"You *what*?" I cried. "You put them in the refrigerator? Why?"

"So they'd be cold," she replied, still grinning.

My sister has a really stupid sense of humour. She has straight, dark brown hair like me. And she's short and a little chubby like me.

"You scared me to death," I told her, sitting up on the bed.

"I know," she replied. She rubbed her hands on my cheeks. They were still cold.

"Yuck. Get away, Mitzi." I shoved her back. "Why did you come up here? Just to scare me?"

She shook her head. "Dad told me to come up. He said to tell you if you're reading comic books instead of doing your homework, you're in big trouble."

She lowered her brown eyes to the comic book, open on the bed. "Guess you're in big trouble, Skipper."

"No. Wait." I grabbed her arm. "This is the new *Masked Mutant*. I *have* to read it! Tell Dad I'm doing my maths, and—"

I didn't finish what I was saying because my dad stepped into the room. The ceiling light reflected in his glasses. But I could still see that he had his eyes on the open comic book on my bed.

"Skipper—" he said angrily in his booming, deep voice.

Mitzi pushed past him and ran out of the room. She liked to cause trouble. But she never wanted to stay around once things got *really* ugly.

And I knew things were about to get ugly— because I had already been warned three times that week about spending too much time with my comic book collection.

"Skipper, do you know why your grades are so bad?" my dad bellowed.

"Because I'm not a very good student?" I replied.

A mistake. Dad hates it when I answer back.

Dad reminds me of a big bear. Not only because he growls a lot. But because he is big and broad. He has short, black hair and almost no forehead. Really. His hair starts almost right above his glasses. And he has a big, booming roar of a voice, like a bear's roar.

Well, after I answered him back, he let out an angry roar. Then he lumbered across the room and picked up my box of comic books—my entire collection.

"Sorry, Skipper, I'm throwing all these out!" he cried, and headed for the door.

You probably expected me to panic. To start begging and pleading for him not to throw away my valuable collection.

But I didn't say anything. I just stood beside the bed with my hands lowered at my sides, and waited.

You see, Dad has done this before. Lots of times. But he doesn't really mean it.

He has a bad temper, but he's no supervillain. Actually, I'd put him in The League of Good Guys most of the time.

His main problem is that he doesn't approve of comic books. He thinks they're just trash. Even when I explain that my collection will probably be worth millions by the time I'm his age.

Anyway, I stood there and waited silently.

Dad stopped at the door and turned around. He held the box in both hands. He narrowed his dark eyes at me through his black-framed glasses.

"Are you going to get to your work?" he asked sternly.

I nodded. "Yes, sir," I muttered, staring at my feet.

He lowered the box a little. It's really heavy, even for a big, strong guy like him. "And you won't waste any more time tonight on comic books?" he demanded.

"Couldn't I just finish this new one?" I asked. I pointed to *The Masked Mutant* comic on the bed.

Another mistake.

He growled at me and turned to carry the box away.

"Okay, okay!" I cried. "Sorry. I'll get my homework done, Dad. I promise. I'll start right now."

He grunted and stepped back into the room. Then he dropped the box back against the wall. "That's all you think about night and day, Skipper," he said quietly. "Comics, comics. It isn't healthy. Really. It isn't."

I didn't say anything. I knew he was about to go back downstairs.

"I don't want to hear any more about comics," Dad said gruffly. "Understand?"

"Okay," I murmured. "Sorry, Dad."

I waited to hear his heavy footsteps going down the stairs. Then I turned back to the new issue of *The Masked Mutant*. I was desperate to find out how SpongeLife escaped from the giant octopus.

But I could hear Mitzi nearby. She was still upstairs. If she saw me reading the comic book, she'd run downstairs and tell Dad for sure. Mitzi's hobby is being a snitch.

So I opened my backpack and started pulling out my maths notebook and my science text book and other stuff I needed.

I zipped through the maths questions as fast as I could. I probably got most of the problems wrong. But it doesn't matter. I'm not any good at maths, anyway.

Then I read the chapter on atoms and molecules in my science text book. Reading about molecules made me think about The Masked Mutant.

I couldn't wait to get back to the comic book.

I finally finished my homework a little after nine-thirty. I had to skip a few essay questions on the literature homework. But only the class brains answer *all* of the questions!

I went downstairs and got myself a bowl of Frosted Flakes, my favourite late-night snack. Then I said good night to my parents and hurried back up to my room, closing the door behind me, eager to get back in bed and start reading.

Back under the ocean. SpongeLife escaped by squishing himself so small, he slipped out of the octopus's tentacles. Pretty cool, I thought.

The Masked Mutant waved his tentacles angrily and vowed he'd get SpongeLife another day. Then he changed his molecules back so he looked like himself, and flew back to his headquarters.

His headquarters!

I stared down at the comic book in shock.

The secret headquarters of The Masked Mutant had never been shown before. Oh, sure, we'd been given glimpses of a room or two on the inside.

But this was the first time the building had ever been shown from the outside.

I brought the page up close to my face and examined it carefully. "What a weird place!" I exclaimed out loud.

The headquarters building didn't look like any building I had ever seen before. It certainly didn't look like the secret hideout of the world's worst villain.

It looked a bit like a giant fire hydrant. A very tall fire hydrant that reached up to the sky. All pink stucco with a huge, green-domed roof.

"Weird," I repeated.

But of course it was the perfect hiding place. Who would ever think that the super bad guy of all time stayed in a building that looked like an enormous pink fire hydrant?

I turned the page. The Masked Mutant slipped

into the building and disappeared into a lift. He rode all the way to the top and stepped out into his private communications centre.

Waiting for him there was . . . a big surprise. A dark figure. We could see only his black silhouette.

But I could tell instantly who it was. It was The Galloping Gazelle, leader of The League of Good Guys.

How did The Gazelle get in? What was he about to do?

To be continued next month.

Wow. I closed the comic. My eyelids felt heavy. My eyes were too tired to read the tiny type on the Letters page. I decided to save it for tomorrow.

Yawning, I carefully set the comic book down on my bed table. I fell asleep before my head hit the pillow.

Two days later, a very cold, clear day, Wilson came running up to me after school. His blue coat was unzipped. He never zipped his coat. He didn't like the way it looked when it was zipped.

I had on a shirt, a sweater, and a heavy, quilted, down coat, zipped up to my chin—and I was still cold. "What's up, Wilson?" I asked.

His breath steamed up in front of him.

"Want to come over and see my rubber stamp collection?"

Was he *kidding*?!

"I have to go to my orthodontist," I told him. "My brace has got comfortable. He has to tighten it so it'll hurt again."

Wilson nodded. His blue eyes matched his coat. "How are you getting there?"

I pointed to the bus stop. "City bus," I told him.

"I've seen you take that bus a lot," he said.

"There's a comic book shop on Goodale Street," I replied, shifting my backpack on to the other shoulder. "I take the bus there once a week or so to see what new comics have come out. The orthodontist is just a few blocks from it."

"Do they have rubber stamps at the comic book store?" Wilson asked.

"I don't think so," I told him. I saw the blue-and-white city bus turn the corner. "Got to run. See you later!" I called.

I turned and ran full speed to the bus stop.

The driver was a nice guy. He saw me running and waited for me. Breathing hard, I thanked him and climbed on to the bus.

I probably wouldn't have thanked him if I had known where this bus was going to take me. But I didn't know that it was carrying me to the most frightening adventure of my life.

The bus was unusually crowded. I stood for a while. Then two people got off, and I slid into a seat.

As the bus bounced along Main Street, I stared out at the passing houses and front yards. Dark clouds hung low over the roofs. I wondered if we were about to get our first snowfall of the winter.

The comic book shop was a few blocks away. I checked my watch, thinking maybe I had time to stop there before my orthodontist appointment. But no. No time for comics today.

"Hey, do you go to Franklin?" A girl's voice interrupted my thoughts.

I turned to see that a girl had taken the seat beside me. Her carrot-coloured hair was tied back in a single plait. She had green eyes and light freckles on her nose.

She wore a heavy, blue-and-red-plaid ski sweater over faded jeans. She held her red canvas backpack in her lap.

17

"Yeah. I go there," I replied.

"How is it?" she asked. She narrowed her green eyes at me as if checking me out.

"It's okay," I told her.

"What's your name?" she asked.

"Skipper," I told her.

She sniggered. "That's not a real name, is it?"

"It's what everyone calls me," I said.

"Do you live on a boat or something?" she asked. Her eyes crinkled up. I could see she was laughing at me.

I guess Skipper is a bit of a stupid name. But I've got used to it. I like it a lot better than my real name—Bradley.

"When I was a little kid, I was always in a hurry," I told her. "So I used to skip a lot. That's why they started calling me Skipper."

"Cute," she replied with a smirk.

I don't think I like this girl, I told myself. "What's your name?" I asked her.

"Skipper," she replied, grinning. "Same as yours."

"No. Really," I insisted.

"It's Libby," she said finally. "Libby Zacks." She stared past me through the window. The bus stopped at a red light. A baby started crying in the back.

"Where are you going?" Libby asked me. "Home?"

I didn't want to tell her I had an orthodontist

18

appointment. That was too geeky. "I'm going to a comic book shop," I said. "The one on Goodale."

"You collect comics?" She sounded surprised. "So do I."

It was my turn to be surprised. Most of the comic book collectors I know are boys. "What kind do you collect?" I asked.

"*High School Harry & Beanhead*," she replied. "I collect all the digest-sized ones and some of the regular ones, too."

"Yuck." I made a face. "High School Harry and his pal Beanhead? Those comics stink."

"They do not!" Libby insisted.

"Those are for babies," I muttered. "They're not real comics."

"They're very well written," Libby replied. "And they're funny." She stuck her tongue out at me. "Maybe you just don't get them."

"Yeah. Maybe," I said, rolling my eyes.

I gazed out of the window. The sky had grown darker. I didn't recognize any of the shops. I saw a restaurant called Pearl's and a tiny barber's shop. Had we passed the comic book shop?

Libby folded her hands over her red backpack. "What do you collect? All that superhero junk?"

"Yeah," I told her. "My collection is worth about a thousand dollars. Maybe two thousand."

"In your dreams," she shot back. She laughed. "*High School Harry* comics never go up in value," I informed her. "Even the Number Ones are worthless. You couldn't get five dollars for your whole collection."

"Why would I want to sell them?" she argued. "I don't want to sell them. And I don't care what they're worth. I just like to read them."

"Then you're not a real collector," I said.

"Are all the boys at Franklin like you?" Libby asked.

"No. I'm the coolest one," I declared.

We both laughed.

I still couldn't decide if I liked her or not. She was pretty cute-looking. And she was funny, in a nasty sort of way.

I stopped laughing when I glanced out of the window and realized I had definitely passed my stop. I saw the bare trees of a small park I'd never seen before. The bus rumbled past it, and more unfamiliar shops came into view.

I felt a sudden stab of panic in my chest. I didn't know this neighbourhood at all.

I pushed the bell and jumped to my feet.

"What's your problem?" Libby demanded.

"My stop. I m-missed it," I stammered.

She moved her legs into the aisle so that I could squeeze past. The bus squealed to a stop. I called out goodbye and hurried through the back door.

Where am I? I asked myself, glancing around. Why did I let myself get into an argument with that girl? Why didn't I pay attention instead?

"Are you lost?" a voice asked.

I turned and saw to my surprise that Libby had followed me off the bus. "What are *you* doing here?" I blurted out.

"It's my stop," she replied. "I live two blocks down that way." She pointed.

"I have to go back," I said, turning to leave.

And as I turned, something came into view that made my breath catch in my throat.

"Ohh." I let out a startled cry and stared across the street. "But—that's *impossible!*" I exclaimed.

I was staring at a tall building on the other corner. A tall, pink stucco building with a bright green, domed roof.

I was staring at the secret headquarters of The Masked Mutant.

"Skipper—what's wrong?" Libby cried.

I couldn't answer her. I stared goggle-eyed at the building across the street. My mouth dropped open. My jaw nearly hit my knees!

I raised my eyes to the bright green roof. Then I slowly lowered them over the shiny pink walls. I had never seen colours like these in real life. They were comic book colours.

It was a comic book building.

But here it was, standing on the corner across the street.

"Skipper? Are you okay?" Libby's voice sounded far away.

It's real! I told myself. The secret headquarters building of The Masked Mutant is real!

Or *is* it?

Two hands shook me by the shoulders, snapping me out of my amazed thoughts. "Skipper! Are you in shock or something?"

"Th-that building!" I stammered.

"Isn't that the ugliest thing you ever saw?" Libby asked, shaking her head. She pushed back her carrot-coloured plait and hiked her backpack on to her shoulder.

"But it—it's—" I still couldn't speak.

"My dad says the architect had to be colour blind," Libby said. "It doesn't even look like a building. It looks like an airship standing on its end."

"How long has it been there?" I asked, my eyes studying the glass doors that were the only entrance.

Libby shrugged. "I don't know. My family only moved here last spring. It was already here."

The clouds darkened overhead. A cold wind swirled around the corner.

"Who do you think works in there?" Libby asked. "There's no sign or anything on the building."

Of *course* there's no sign, I thought. It's the secret headquarters of the world's most evil villain. There's no way The Masked Mutant would put a sign out the front!

He doesn't want The League of Good Guys to find his secret headquarters, I told myself.

"This is crazy," I cried.

I turned and saw Libby staring at me. "You sure you're okay? It's just a building, Skipper. No need to go ballistic."

I could feel my face turning red. Libby must think I'm some kind of a nut, I realized. "I—I think I've seen this building somewhere before," I tried to explain.

"I've got to get home," she said, glancing up at the darkening sky. "Want to come round? I'll show you my comic book collection."

"No. I'm late for my orthodontist appointment," I replied.

"Huh?" She narrowed her green eyes at me. "You said you were going to a comic book shop."

I could feel my face turning even redder. "Uh . . . I'm going to the comic book shop *after* my appointment," I told her.

"How long have you had your brace?" she asked.

I groaned. "For ever."

She started backing away. "Well, see you sometime."

"Yeah. Bye."

She turned and jogged down the street. She must think I'm a total geek, I thought unhappily.

But I couldn't help it. I really was in shock, seeing that building. I turned back to it. The top of the building had become hidden by the lowering clouds. Now the building looked like a sleek, pink rocket ship, reaching up to the clouds.

A moving truck rumbled past. I waited for it to go by, then hurried across the street.

There was no one on the pavement. I hadn't seen anyone go into the building or come out of it.

It's just a big office building, I told myself. Nothing to get excited about.

But my heart was pounding as I stopped a few feet from the glass doors at the entrance. I took a deep breath and peeked in.

I know it's crazy, but I really expected to see people wearing superhero costumes walking around in there.

I narrowed my eyes and squinted through the glass doors.

I couldn't see anyone. It appeared dark inside.

I took a step closer. Then another.

I brought my face right up to the glass and peered in. I could see a wide lobby. Pink-and-yellow walls. A row of lifts near the back.

But no people. No one. Empty.

I grabbed the glass-door handle. My throat made a loud gulping sound as I swallowed hard.

Should I go in? I asked myself. Do I dare?

My hand tightened on the glass-door handle. I started to tug the heavy door open.

Then, out of the corner of my eye, I saw a blue-and-white bus moving towards me. I glanced at my watch. I was only five minutes late for my appointment. If I jumped on the bus, I could be at the orthodontist's office in a few minutes.

Letting go of the handle, I turned and ran to the bus stop, my backpack bouncing on my shoulders. I felt disappointed. But I also felt relieved.

Walking into the headquarters of the meanest mutant in the universe was a little scary.

The bus eased to a stop. I waited for an elderly man to step off. Then I climbed on board, dropped my money into the box, and hurried to the back of the bus.

I wanted to get one last look at the mysterious pink-and-green building.

Two women were sitting in the back seat. But I pushed between them and pressed my face against the back window.

As the bus pulled away, I stared at the building. Its colours stayed bright, even though the sky was so dark behind it. The pavement was empty. I still hadn't seen anyone come out or go inside.

A few seconds later, the building disappeared into the distance. I turned away from the window and walked up the aisle to find a seat.

Weird, I thought. Totally weird.

"And it was the exact same building as in the comic book?" Wilson asked. His blue eyes stared across the lunchroom table at me.

I nodded. "As soon as I got home yesterday afternoon, I checked out the comic book. The building was exactly the same."

Wilson pulled a sandwich from his lunch bag and started to unwrap the foil. "What kind of sandwich did your mum pack for you?" he asked.

I opened mine. "Tuna salad. What's yours?"

He lifted a slice of bread and examined his sandwich. "Tuna salad," he replied. "Want to swap?"

"We both have tuna salad," I told him. "Why do you want to swap?"

He shrugged. "I don't know."

We swapped sandwiches. His mum's tuna salad was better than mine. I pulled the juice carton from my lunch bag. Then I threw the apple in the bin. I keep telling Mum not to pack an apple. I told her I just threw it away every day. Why does she keep packing one?

"Can I have your pudding container?" I asked Wilson.

"No," he replied.

I finished the first half of the sandwich. I was thinking hard about the mysterious building. I'd been thinking about it ever since I saw it.

"I've solved the mystery," Wilson said. He scratched his white-blond curls. A smile formed on his face. "Yes! I've solved it!"

"What?" I demanded eagerly.

"It's simple," Wilson replied. "Who draws The Masked Mutant?"

"The artist?" I asked. "Jimmy Starenko, of course. Starenko *created* The Masked Mutant and The League of Good Guys." How could Wilson not know that?

"Well, I'll bet this guy Starenko was here one day," Wilson continued, jabbing the straw into the top of his juice carton.

"Starenko? Here? In Riverview Falls?" I said. I wasn't following him.

Wilson nodded. "Let's say Starenko is here. He's driving down the street, and he sees the weird building. He stops his car. He gets out. He

28

stares at the building. And he thinks: What a great building! This building would make a perfect secret headquarters building for The Masked Mutant."

"Wow. I see," I murmured. I was catching on to Wilson's thinking. "You mean, he saw the building, liked it, and copied it when he drew the headquarters building."

Wilson nodded. He had a piece of celery stuck to his front tooth. "Yeah. Maybe he got out of the car and sketched the building. Then he kept the sketches in a drawer or something till he needed them."

It made sense.

Actually, it made too much sense. I felt really disappointed. I knew it was silly, but I really *wanted* that building to be The Masked Mutant's secret headquarters.

Wilson had spoiled everything. Why did he have to be so sensible for once?

"I've got some new rubber stamps," he told me, finishing the last spoonful from his pudding container. "Want to see them? I could bring them over to your house after school."

"No thanks," I replied. "That would be *too* exciting."

I planned to take the bus and go to see the building again that afternoon. But Ms Partridge gave us a ton of homework. I had to go straight home.

The next day, it snowed. Wilson and I and some other guys went tobogganing on Grover's Hill.

A week later, I finally had a chance to go back and take another look at the building. This time, I'm going inside, I told myself. There must be a receptionist or a guard, I decided. I'll ask whose building it is and who works there.

I was feeling really brave as I climbed on to the bus after school. It was an ordinary office building, after all. Nothing to get excited about.

Taking a seat at the front of the bus, I looked for Libby. The bus was filled with kids going home after school. Near the back, I saw a red-haired girl arguing with another girl. But it wasn't Libby.

No sign of her.

I stared out of the window as the bus rolled past the comic book shop. Then, a few blocks later, we bounced past my orthodontist's office. Just seeing his building made my teeth ache!

It was a sunny, clear afternoon. Bright sunlight kept filling the bus windows, forcing me to shield my eyes as I stared out.

I had to keep careful watch, because I wasn't sure where the stop was. I really didn't know this neighbourhood at all.

Kids were jammed in the aisle. So I couldn't

see out of the windows on the other side of the bus.

I hope we haven't already passed the building, I thought. I had a heavy feeling in the pit of my stomach. I have a real fear of getting lost.

My mum says that when I was two, she lost me for a few minutes in the frozen foods section at the supermarket. I think I've had a fear of getting lost ever since.

The bus pulled up to a bus stop. I recognized the small park across the street. This was the stop!

"Getting off!" I shouted, jumping into the aisle. I hit a boy with my backpack as I stumbled to the front door. "Sorry. Getting off! Getting off!"

I pushed through the crowd of kids and leaped down the steps, on to the kerb. The bus rumbled away. Sunlight streamed around me.

I stepped to the corner. Yes. This was the right stop. I recognized it all now.

I turned and raised my eyes to the strange building.

And found myself staring at a large, empty lot.

The building was gone.

"Whoa!" I cried, frozen in shock.

Shielding my eyes with one hand, I stared across the street. How could that enormous building vanish in one week?

I didn't have long to think about it. Another bus pulled up to the bus stop. "Skipper! Hey—Skipper!" Libby hopped off the bus, waving and calling my name.

She was wearing the same red-and-blue ski sweater and faded jeans, torn at one knee. Her hair was pulled straight back, tied in a ponytail with a blue hair scrunchie.

"Hey—what are you doing back in *my* neighbourhood?" she asked, smiling as she ran over to me.

"Th-that building!" I stammered, pointing to the vacant lot. "It's gone!"

Libby's expression changed. "Well, don't say hi or anything," she muttered, frowning at me.

"Hi," I said. "What happened to that building?"

She turned and followed my stare. Then she shrugged. "Guess they've knocked it down."

"But—but—" I sputtered.

"It was so ugly," Libby said. "Maybe the city *made* them knock it down."

"But did you *see* them knock it down?" I demanded impatiently. "You live near here, right? Did you see them doing it?"

She thought about it, crinkling her green eyes as she thought. "Well . . . no," she replied finally. "I've gone past here a few times, but—"

"You didn't see any machinery?" I demanded anxiously. "Any big wrecking balls? Any bulldozers? Dozens of workers?"

Libby shook her head. "No. I didn't actually see anyone knocking the building down. But I didn't really look."

She pulled her red backpack off her shoulder and held the strap in front of her with both hands. "I don't know *why* you're so interested in that ugly building, Skipper. I'm glad it's gone."

"But it was in a comic book!" I blurted out.

"Huh?" She stared hard at me. "What are you talking about?"

I knew she wouldn't understand. "Nothing," I muttered.

"Skipper, did you come all the way out here just to see that building?" she asked.

"No way," I lied. "Of course not."

"Do you want to come to my house and see my comic book collection?"

I was so frazzled and mixed up, I said yes.

I hurried out of Libby's house less than an hour later. Those *High School Harry & Beanhead* comics are the most boring comics in the world! And the art is so lame. Can't everyone see that the two girls are drawn exactly the same, except one has blonde hair and one has black?

Yuck!

Libby insisted on showing me every *High School Harry & Beanhead* comic she had. And she had shelves full of them!

Of course I couldn't concentrate on those boring comics. I couldn't stop thinking about the weird building. How could a whole building vanish without a trace?

I jogged back to the bus stop on Main Street. The sun was sinking behind the buildings. Long blue shadows tilted over the pavements.

When I get to the corner, I bet the building will be back! I found myself thinking.

But of course it wasn't.

I know. I know. I have weird thoughts. I guess it comes from reading too many comic books.

I had to wait nearly half an hour for the bus to come. I spent the whole time staring at the empty lot, thinking about the vanished building.

When I finally got home, I found a brown envelope waiting for me on the little table in the hall where Mum drops the mail.

"Yes!" I exclaimed happily. The special issue of *The Masked Mutant*! The comics company was sending out two special editions this month, and this was the first.

I called "hi" to my mum, tossed my coat and heavy backpack on to the floor, and raced up the stairs to my room, the comic book gripped tightly in my hot little hand.

I couldn't wait to see what had happened after The Galloping Gazelle sneaked into The Masked Mutant's headquarters. Carefully, I slid the comic book out of the envelope and examined the cover.

And there it stood. The pink-and-green headquarters building. Right on the cover.

My hand trembled as I opened to the first page. *MORNING OF A MUTANT* was the big title in scary red letters. The Masked Mutant stood in front of a big communications console.

He stared into a wall of about Twenty TV monitors. Each TV monitor showed a different member of The League of Good Guys.

"I'm tracking each one of them," The Masked Mutant said in the first dialogue balloon. "They'll never find me. I've thrown an Invisibility Curtain around my entire headquarters!"

My mouth dropped open as I read those words.

I read them three times before I let the comic book slip out of my hands to my bed.

An Invisibility Curtain.

No one can see The Masked Mutant's building because he's slipped an Invisibility Curtain around it.

I sat excitedly on the edge of my bed, breathing hard, feeling the blood pulse at my temples.

Is that what happened in real life?

Is that why I couldn't see the pink-and-green building this afternoon?

Was the comic book giving me the answer to the mystery of the missing building?

It sounded crazy. It sounded *totally* crazy.

But was it real? Was there *really* an Invisibility Curtain hiding the building?

My head was spinning faster than The Amazing Tornado-Man! I knew only one thing. I had to go back there and find out.

After school the next afternoon, I had to go with my mum to the shops to buy trainers. I usually try on at least ten or twelve pairs, then beg for the most expensive ones. You know. The ones that pump up or flash lights when you walk in them.

But this time I bought the first pair I saw, plain black-and-white Reeboks. I mean, who could think about trainers when an invisible building was waiting to be discovered?

Driving home from the shops, I started to tell Mum about the building. But she stopped me after a few sentences. "I wish you were as interested in your schoolwork as you are in those stupid comics," she said, sighing.

That's what she always says.

"When is the last time you read a good book?" she continued.

That's the *next* thing she always says.

I decided to change the subject. "We dissected

a worm today for science," I told her.

She made a disgusted face. "Doesn't your teacher have anything better to do than to cut up poor, innocent worms?"

There was just no pleasing Mum today.

The next afternoon, wearing my new trainers, I eagerly hopped on the city bus. Tossing my token into the box, I saw Libby sitting near the back. As the bus lurched away from the kerb, I stumbled down the aisle and dropped beside her, lowering my backpack to the floor.

"I'm going back to that building," I said breathlessly. "I think there's an Invisibility Curtain around it."

"Don't you ever say hi?" she complained, rolling her eyes.

I said hi. Then I repeated what I had said about the Invisibility Curtain. I told her I'd read about it in the newest *Masked Mutant* comic, and that the comic may be giving clues as to what was happening in real life.

Libby listened to me intently, not blinking, not moving. I could see that she was finally starting to see why I was so excited about finding this building.

When I finished explaining everything, she put a hand on my forehead. "You don't *feel* hot," she said. "Are you seeing a shrink?"

"Huh?" I pushed her hand away.

"Are you seeing a shrink? You're totally out of your mind. You know that—don't you?"

"I'm not crazy," I said. "I'll prove it. Come with me."

She edged closer to the window, as if trying to get away from me. "No way," she declared. "I can't believe I'm sitting here with a boy who thinks that comic books come to life."

She pointed out of the window. "Hey, look, Skipper—there goes the Easter Bunny! He's handing an egg to the Tooth Fairy!" She laughed. A mean laugh.

"Ha-ha," I muttered angrily. I have a good sense of humour. But I don't like being laughed at by girls who collect *High School Harry & Beanhead* comics.

The bus pulled up to the bus stop. I hoisted my backpack and scrambled out of the back exit. Libby stepped off right behind me.

As the bus pulled away, sending out puffs of black exhaust behind it, I gazed across the street.

No building. An empty lot.

"Well?" I turned to Libby. "You coming?"

She twisted her mouth into a thoughtful expression. "To that empty lot? Skipper, aren't you going to feel like a jerk when there's nothing there?"

"Well, go home then," I told her sharply.

"Okay. I'll come," she said, grinning.

We crossed the street. Two teenagers on bikes nearly ran us over. "Missed 'em!" one of them cried. The other one laughed.

"How do we get through the Invisibility Curtain?" Libby asked. Her voice sounded serious. But I could see by her eyes that she was laughing at me.

"In the comic book, people just stepped through it," I told her. "You can't feel it or anything. It's like a smoke screen. But once you step through it, you can see the building."

"Okay. Let's try it," Libby said. She tossed her ponytail over her shoulder. "Let's get this over with, okay?"

Walking side by side, we took a step across the pavement towards the empty lot. Then another step. Then another.

We crossed the pavement and stepped on to the hard dirt.

"I can't believe I'm doing this," Libby grumbled. We took another step. "I can't believe I'm—"

She stopped because the building popped into view.

"Ohhh!" We both cried out in unison. She grabbed my wrist and squeezed it hard. Her hand was ice-cold.

We stood a few feet from the glass entrance. The bright walls of the pink-and-green building rose above us.

"You—you were right!" Libby stammered, still squeezing my wrist.

I swallowed hard. I tried to talk, but my mouth was suddenly too dry. I coughed, and no words came out.

"Now what?" Libby asked, staring up at the shiny walls.

I still couldn't speak.

The comic book is *real*! I thought. The comic book is real.

Does that mean the building really belongs to The Masked Mutant?

Whoa! I warned myself to slow down. My heart was already racing faster than Speedboy.

"Now what?" Libby repeated impatiently. "Let's get *away* from here—okay?" For the first time, she sounded really frightened.

"No way!" I told her. "Come on. Let's go in."

She tugged me back. "Go in? Are you *crazy*?"

"We have to," I told her. "Come on. Don't stop to think about it. Let's go."

I took a deep breath, pulled open the heavy glass door, and we slipped inside.

We took one step into the brightly-lit lobby. My heart was pounding so hard, my chest hurt. My knees were shaking. I'd never been so scared in my life!

I glanced quickly all around.

The lobby was enormous. It seemed to stretch on for ever. The pink-and-yellow walls gave off a soft glow. The sparkly white ceiling seemed to be a mile above our heads.

I didn't see a reception desk. No chairs or tables. No furniture of any kind.

"Where *is* everyone?" Libby whispered. I could see that she was frightened, too. She clung to my arm, standing close beside me.

The vast room was empty. Not another person in sight.

I took another step.

And heard a soft *beep*.

A beam of yellow light shot out of the wall and rolled down over my body.

I felt a gentle tingling. Kind of a prickly feeling, the kind of feeling when your arm goes to sleep.

It swept down quickly from my head to my feet. A second or two later, the light vanished and the tingly feeling went away.

"What was *that*?" I whispered to Libby.

"What was *what*?" she replied.

"Didn't you feel that?"

She shook her head. "I didn't feel anything. Are you trying to scare me or something, Skipper?"

"It was some kind of electric beam," I told her. "It shone on me when I stepped forward."

"Let's get out of here," she muttered. "It's so quiet, it's creepy."

I turned my eyes to the row of lifts against the yellow wall. Did I dare take a ride on one? Was I brave enough to do a little exploring?

"It—it's just a big office building," I told Libby, trying to work up my courage.

"Well, if it's an office building, where are the workers?" she demanded.

"Maybe the offices are closed," I suggested.

"On a Thursday?" Libby replied. "It isn't a holiday or anything. I think the building is empty, Skipper. I don't think anyone works here."

I took a few steps towards the lifts. My trainers thudded loudly on the hard marble floor. "But all the lights are on, Libby," I said. "And the door was open."

She hurried to catch up with me. Her eyes kept darting back and forth. I could see she was really scared.

"I know what you're thinking," she said. "You don't think this is just an office building. You think this is the secret headquarters of that comic book character—don't you, Skipper?"

I swallowed hard. My knees were still shaking. I tried to make them stop, but they wouldn't.

"Well, maybe it is," I replied, staring at the lifts across from us. "I mean, how do you explain the Invisibility Curtain? It was in the comic book—and it was outside this building."

"I—I can't explain it," Libby stammered. "It's weird. It's *too* weird. This place gives me the creeps, Skipper. I really think—"

"There's only one way to find out the truth," I said. I tried to sound brave, but my voice shook nearly as much as my knees!

Libby followed my gaze to the lifts. She guessed what I was thinking. "No way!" she cried, stepping back towards the glass doors.

"We'll just ride up and down," I told her. "Maybe open the lift doors on a few floors and peek out."

"No way," Libby repeated. Her face suddenly appeared very pale. Her green eyes were wide with fright.

"Libby, it will only take a minute," I insisted. "We've come this far. I have to explore a little. I don't want to go home without finding out what this building is."

"*You* can ride the lifts," she said. "I'm going home." She backed up to the glass doors.

Outside I saw a blue-and-white bus stop at the kerb. A woman climbed off, carrying a baby in one hand, dragging a pushchair in the other.

I could run out of the door and climb right on to that bus, I thought. I could get out of here, safe and sound. And be on my way home.

But what would happen when I got home?

I would feel like a coward, a total wimp. And I would spend day after day wondering about this building, wondering if I had actually discovered the secret headquarters of a real supervillain.

If I jumped on the bus and rode home now, the building would still be a mystery. And the mystery would drive me crazy.

"Okay, Libby, you can go home if you want," I told her. "I'm going to take the lift to the top and back."

She stared at me thoughtfully. Then she rolled her eyes. "Okay, okay. I'll come with you," she murmured, shaking her head.

I was glad. I really didn't want to go alone.

"I'm only doing this because I feel sorry for you," Libby said, following me across the marble floor to the lifts.

45

"Huh? Why do you feel sorry for me?" I demanded.

"Because you're so messed up," she replied. "You really think a comic book can come to life. That's sad. That's really sad."

"Thank goodness High School Harry and Beanhead can't come to life!" I teased. Then I added, "What about the Invisibility Curtain? That was real—wasn't it?"

Libby didn't reply. Instead, she laughed. "You're serious about this!" she said. The sound of her laughter echoed in the enormous, empty lobby.

It made me feel a little braver. I laughed, too.

What's the big deal? I asked myself. So you're going to take a lift ride. So what?

It's not like The Masked Mutant is going to jump into the lift with us, I assured myself. We'll probably peek out at a lot of boring offices. And that's all.

I pushed the lighted button on the wall. Instantly, the silvery lift door in front of us slid open.

I poked my head into the lift. It had walls of dark brown wood with a silver railing that went all the way around.

There were no signs on the walls. No building directory. No words at all.

I suddenly realized there were no signs in the lobby, either. Not even a sign with the name of the building. Or a sign to tell visitors where to check in.

Weird.

"Let's go," I said.

Libby held back. I tugged her by the arm into the lift.

The doors slid shut silently behind us as soon as we stepped in. I turned to the control panel to the left of the door. It was a long, silvery rectangle filled with buttons.

I pushed the button to the top floor.

The lift started to hum. It jerked slightly as we began to move.

I turned to Libby. She had her back pressed against the wall, her hands shoved into her jeans pockets. She stared straight ahead at the door.

"We're moving," I murmured.

The lift picked up speed.

"Hey!" Libby and I both cried out at the same time.

"We—we're going *down*!" I exclaimed.

I had pushed the button to the top floor. But we were dropping. Fast.

Faster.

I grabbed the railing with both hands.

Where was it taking us?

Would it ever stop?

The lift stopped with a hard *thud* that made my knees bend. "Whoa!" I cried.

I let go of the railing and turned to Libby beside me. "You okay?"

She nodded. She stared straight ahead at the lift door.

"We should have gone up," I muttered tensely. "I pushed *up*."

"Why doesn't the door open?" Libby asked in a trembling voice.

We both stared at the door. I stepped to the centre of the lift. "Open!" I commanded it.

The door didn't move.

"We're trapped in here," Libby said, her voice getting shrill and tiny.

"No," I replied, still trying to be the brave one. "It'll open. Watch. It's just slow."

The door didn't open.

"The lift must be broken," Libby wailed. "We'll be trapped down here for ever. The air is starting to run out already. I can't breathe!"

"Don't panic," I warned, struggling to keep my voice calm. "Take a deep breath, Libby. There's plenty of air."

She obediently sucked in a deep breath. She let it out in a long *whoosh*. "Why won't the door open? I *knew* we shouldn't have done this!"

I turned to the control panel. A button at the bottom read OPEN. I pushed it. Instantly, the door slid open.

I turned back to Libby. "See? We're okay."

"But where *are* we?" she cried.

I stepped to the doorway and poked my head out. It was very dark. I could see some kind of heavy machinery in the darkness.

"We're in the basement, I think," I told Libby. "There are all kinds of pipes and a big boiler and things."

"Let's go," Libby urged, hanging back against the wall of the lift.

I took a step out of the door and glanced both ways. I couldn't see much. More machinery. A row of metal bins. A stack of long metal boxes.

"Come on, Skipper," Libby demanded. "Let's go back up. Now!"

I stepped back into the elevator and pushed the button marked LOBBY.

The door didn't close. The lift didn't move, didn't hum.

I pushed LOBBY again. I pushed it five or six times.

Nothing happened.

I suddenly had a lump in my throat as big as a watermelon. I really didn't want to be stuck down in this dark basement.

I started pushing buttons wildly. I pushed everything. I pushed a red button marked EMERGENCY five or six times.

Nothing.

"I don't *believe* this!" I choked out.

"Let's get out and take a different lift," Libby suggested.

Good idea, I thought. There was a long row of lifts up in the lobby. We'll just get out of this one and push the button for another one to come down and get us.

I led the way out into the dark basement. Libby stayed close behind me.

"Oh!" We both let out low cries as the lift door quickly slid shut behind us.

"What's going on?" I demanded. "Why wouldn't it close before?"

Libby didn't reply.

I waited for my eyes to adjust to the darkness. Then I saw what Libby was staring at.

"Where are the other lifts?" she cried.

We were staring at a smooth, bare wall. The lift that had brought us down here was the only lift on the wall.

I spun around, checking out the other walls. But it was too dark to see very far.

"The other lifts don't come down here, I guess," Libby murmured in a trembling voice.

I searched the wall for a button to push to bring our lift back. I couldn't find one. No button.

"There's no way out!" Libby wailed. "No way out at all!"

"Maybe there are lifts on the other wall," I said, pointing across the huge, dark room.

"Maybe," Libby repeated doubtfully.

"Maybe there's a staircase or something," I said.

"Maybe," she said softly.

A sudden noise made me jump. A rumble followed by a grinding hum.

"Just the boiler starting up," I told Libby.

"Let's find a way out of here," she urged. "I'm never going in a lift again as long as I live!"

I could feel her hand on my shoulder as I started to make my way through the darkness. The huge, grey boiler rumbled and coughed. Another big machine made a soft clattering sound as we edged past it.

"Anybody down here?" I called. My voice echoed off the long, dust-covered pipes that ran along the low ceiling above our heads. I cupped my hands around my mouth and called again. "Anybody here? Can anybody hear me?"

Silence.

The only sounds I could hear were the rumble of the boiler and the soft scrape of our trainers as Libby and I slowly crept over the floor.

As we came near the far wall, we could see that there were no lifts over here. The smooth plaster wall was bare except for a thick tangle of cobwebs up near the ceiling.

"There's *got* to be some stairs leading out of here," Libby whispered, close behind me.

Dim light shone through a narrow doorway up ahead. "Let's see where this leads," I said, brushing stringy spiderwebs off my face.

We stepped through the doorway and found ourselves in a long hallway. Dust-covered ceiling bulbs cast pale light on to the concrete floor.

"Anybody here?" I called again. My voice sounded hollow in the long tunnel of a hallway.

No reply.

Dark doorways lined both sides of the hallway. I peeked into each door as we passed. I saw stacks of boxes, tall filing cabinets, strange machinery I didn't recognize. One large room was jammed with enormous coils of metal cable. Another room had sheets of metal piled nearly to the ceiling.

"Helloooooo!" I called. "Helllllooooooo!"

No reply.

Flashing red lights inside a large room caught my eye. I stopped at the doorway and stared in at some sort of control panel.

One wall was filled with blinking red and green lights. In front of the lights stood a long counter of dials and gears and levers. Three tall stools were placed along the counter. But no one was sitting in them.

No one was working the controls. The room was empty. As empty as the rest of this strange, frightening basement.

"Weird, huh?" I whispered to Libby.

When she didn't answer, I turned to make sure she was okay.

"Libby?"

She was gone.

13

I spun around. "Libby?"

My entire body shook.

"Where are you?"

I squinted back down the long, grey hallway.
No sign of her.

"Libby? If this is some kind of a stupid joke ..."
I started. But the rest of my words caught in my
throat.

Breathing hard, I forced myself to retrace our
steps. "Libby?" I stopped at every door and
called her name. "Libby?"

The hallway curved, and I followed it. I began
jogging, my hands down stiffly at my sides,
calling her name, searching every door, peering
into every dark room.

How could she get lost? I asked myself, feeling
my panic rise until I could barely breathe. She
was right behind me.

I turned another corner. Into a hallway I
hadn't explored yet. "Libby?"

The narrow hall led to an enormous, brightly-lit room. I had to shut my eyes against the sudden bright light.

When I opened them, I found myself nearly face-to-face with a gigantic machine. Bright floodlights from the high ceiling covered it in light.

The machine had to be a block long! A big control panel, filled with dials, and buttons, and lights, stood against the side. A long, flat part—like a conveyor belt—led to several rollers. And at the very end of the machine stood a huge white wheel. No—a cylinder. No—a roll of white paper.

It's a printing press! I realized.

I lurched into the room, stepping around stacks of paper and cardboard boxes. The floor was littered with paper, ink-smeared paper, crumpled, folded, and ripped.

As I staggered towards the huge printing press, the sea of paper rose up nearly to my knees!

"Libby? Are you in here? Libby?"

Silence.

This room was as empty as all the others.

The paper crackled under my trainers. I made my way to a long table at the back of the room. I found a red stool in front of the table, and I dropped down on it.

I kicked big sheets of paper away from my legs

and glanced around the room. A hundred questions pushed into my mind at once.

Where is Libby? How could she disappear like that?

Is she somewhere close behind me? Will she follow the hallway to this big room?

Where is everyone? Why is this place totally deserted?

Is this where they print the comic books? Am I in the basement of Collectable Comics, the company that publishes *The Masked Mutant*?

Questions, questions.

My brain felt about to burst. I stared around the cluttered room, my eyes rolling past the gigantic printing press, searching for Libby.

Where was she? *Where?*

I turned back to the table—and gasped.

I nearly toppled off the stool. The Masked Mutant was staring up at me.

A large, colour drawing of The Masked Mutant stared at me from the table. Startled, I picked it up and examined it.

It had been drawn on thick posterboard in coloured inks. The Masked Mutant's cape swept behind him. Through his mask, his eyes appeared to stare out at me. Evil, angry eyes.

The ink glistened on the page, as if still wet. I rubbed my thumb over an edge of the cape. The ink didn't come off.

I wonder if Starenko drew this portrait, I thought, studying it.

Glancing across the table, I saw a stack of papers on a low counter that ran along the entire back wall. Hopping off the tall stool, I made my way over to the counter and began shuffling through the papers.

They were ink drawings and pencil sketches. Many of them were of The Masked Mutant. They showed him in different poses. Some of them showed him moving his molecules around, changing into wild animals and strange, unearthly creatures.

I opened a thick folder and found about a dozen colour sketches of the members of The League of Good Guys. Then I found a stack of pencil drawings of characters I'd never seen before.

This *must* be where they make the comic books! I told myself.

I was so excited about seeing these actual drawings and sketches, I nearly forgot about Libby.

This pink-and-green building must be the headquarters of Collectable Comics, I realized.

I was starting to feel calmer. My fears dropped away like feathers off The Battling Bird-Boy.

After all, there was nothing to be afraid of. I hadn't stumbled into the headquarters of the world's most evil supervillain. I was in the basement of the comic book offices.

This is where the writers and artists worked. And this is where they print the comic books every month.

So why should I be afraid?

I shuffled through folder after folder, making my way down the long counter. I found a pile of layouts for a comic book that I had just bought.

It was so exciting seeing the actual art. The page was really big, at least twice as big as the comic book. I guessed that the artists made their drawings much bigger than the actual page. And then they shrank the drawings down when they printed them.

I found some really new pencil drawings of The Masked Mutant. I knew they were new because I didn't recognize them from my comics at home—and I have them all!

Drawing after drawing. My eyes were practically spinning!

I never dreamed that Collectable Comics were made right in Riverview Falls.

I flipped through a sketchbook of Penguin People portraits. I never liked the Penguin People. I know they're good guys, and people really think they're great. But I think their black-and-white costumes just look silly.

I was having a great time. Really enjoying myself.

Of course it had to end.

It ended when I opened the last folder on the counter. And stared at the sketches inside.

I gaped at them in disbelief, my hands trembling as I shuffled down from one to the next.

"This is impossible!" I cried out loud.

I was staring at sketches of ME.

I frantically shuffled through the big stack of drawings.

You're just imagining it, Skipper, I told myself. The boy in the sketches only looks like you. It isn't really you.

But it *had* to be me.

In every drawing, the boy had my round face, my dark hair—cut short on the sides and long on top.

He was short like me. And just a little bit chubby. He had my crooked smile, up a little higher on one side. He wore my clothes—baggy jeans and long-sleeved, pocket T-shirts.

I stopped at a drawing halfway through the pile and stared hard at it, holding it close to my face. "Oh, wow!" I exclaimed.

The boy in the drawing even had a chip in his front tooth. Just like me.

"It's impossible!" I cried out loud, my voice tiny and shrill in the enormous room.

Who had been drawing me? And why? Why would a comic book artist make sketch after sketch of me?

And how did the artist know me so well? How did the artist know that I have a tiny chip in one front tooth?

A cold shiver ran down my back. I suddenly felt very frightened. I stared at the drawings, my heart pounding.

In one drawing, I looked really scared. I was running from something, my arms out stiffly in front of me.

Another drawing was a close-up portrait of my face. My expression in the sketch was angry. No. More than angry. I looked furious.

Another sketch showed me flexing my muscles. Hey, I look pretty cool! I thought. The artist had given me bulging superhero biceps.

In another drawing, my eyes were closed. Was I asleep? Or was I dead?

I was still staring at the drawings, shuffling from one to the next, studying each one—when I heard the footsteps.

And realized I was no longer alone.

"Who-who's there?" I cried, whirling around.

"Where *were* you?" Libby demanded angrily, running across the room towards me. "I searched everywhere!"

"Where were *you*?" I shot back. "I thought you were right behind me."

"I thought you were right *ahead* of me!" she cried. "I turned a corner, and you were gone." She stopped in front of me, breathing hard, her face bright red. "How could you leave me by myself in this creepy place?"

"I didn't!" I insisted. "You left *me*!"

She shook her head, still gasping for breath. "Well, let's get *out* of here, Skipper. I've found some lifts that are working." She tugged my sleeve.

I picked up the stack of drawings. "Look, Libby." I held them up to her. "You have to see these."

"Are you serious?" she cried. "I want to get *out*

of here. I don't want to look at comic book drawings now!"

"But—but—" I sputtered, waving the drawings.

She turned and started towards the doorway. "I *told* you I've found some lifts. Are you coming or not?"

"But these are drawings of *me*!" I cried.

"Yeah. Sure," she called back sarcastically. She stopped at the front of the big printing press and turned back to me. "Why would anyone draw *you*, Skipper?"

"I-I don't know," I stammered. "But these drawings—"

"You have a sick imagination," she said. "You seem like a normal guy. But you're totally weird. Bye." Libby started jogging over the paper-cluttered floor to the door.

"No—wait!" I called. I dropped the drawings on to the counter, slid off the tall stool, and chased after her. "Wait up, Libby!"

I followed her out into the hall. I didn't want to be left alone in this creepy place, either. I had to get home and think about this. I had to puzzle it out.

My head was spinning. I felt totally confused.

I followed her through the long tunnel of hallways. We turned a corner, and I saw a row of lifts against the wall.

Libby pushed the button on the wall, and one

of the lifts slid open silently. We both peered carefully inside before stepping in. It was empty.

We were both panting. My head was throbbing. My side ached. Neither of us spoke a word.

Libby pushed the button marked LOBBY. We heard a soft hum and felt the lift start to move.

When the door slid open, and we saw the pink-and-yellow walls of the lobby, Libby and I both cheered. We burst out of the lift together and ran across the marble floor to the exit.

Out on the pavement, I stopped, lowering my hands to my knees, sucking in deep breaths of fresh air. When I glanced up, I saw Libby studying her watch.

"I've got to get home," she said. "My mum is going to have a cow!"

"Do you believe me about the drawings?" I asked breathlessly.

"No," she replied. "Who would believe *that*?" She waved and made her way across the street, heading for home.

I could see a bus approaching, a few blocks down. Searching in my jeans pocket for some change, I turned to take one last look at the weird building.

It had vanished once again.

I needed time to think about everything that had happened. But Wilson was waiting for me when

I got home, and he followed me up to my room.

"I brought over some of my rubber stamps," he said, raising a brown paper bag up to my face. He turned it over and emptied it on to my desk. "I thought you might like to see some of the better ones."

"Wilson—" I started. "I really don't—"

"This one is a ladybird," he said, holding up a small wooden stamp. "It's very old. It's the oldest one I own. Here. I'll show it to you." He opened a blue inkpad, stamped the ladybird on it, and pressed it on to the top of a pad of paper I had on the desk.

"How old is it?" I asked him.

"I don't know," he replied. He held up another one. "It's a cow," he said. As if I couldn't tell. He stamped it on to the pad. "I have several cows," Wilson said. "But I only brought one."

I studied the cow, pretending to be interested.

"It's another really old one," Wilson said proudly.

"How old?" I asked.

He shrugged. "Beats me." He reached for another stamp.

"Uh . . . Wilson . . . I just had a really weird thing happen," I told him. "And I need to think about it. Alone."

He narrowed his blue eyes at me, confused. "What happened?"

"It's a bit of a long story," I said. "I was in a

building. On the north side of town. I think it's where they make the Collectable Comics."

"Really? Here in Riverview Falls?" Wilson's face filled with surprise. "And they let you in?"

"There was no one there," I told him. It felt good to share the story with someone. "So we went in. This girl I met on the bus. Libby. And me. We tried to go up in the lift. But it took us down. Then Libby got lost. And I found a stack of drawings of myself."

"Whoa!" Wilson exclaimed, raising a hand for me to stop. "I'm not following this too well, Skipper."

I realized what I had said didn't make any sense at all. How could I explain it?

I told Wilson I'd talk to him later, after I'd calmed down. I helped him gather up his rubber stamps. He'd brought about twenty of them. "Twenty of the best," he said.

I walked him downstairs and said I'd call him after dinner.

After he left, something caught my eye on the mail table in the hall. A brown envelope.

My heart jumped. Was it—? Yes! An envelope from the Collectable Comics company. The next special issue of *The Masked Mutant*.

I was so excited, I nearly knocked the whole table over as I grabbed for the envelope. I tucked it under my arm without opening it and ran up the stairs, two at a time.

I need total privacy. I have to study this! I told myself.

I closed the bedroom door behind me and dropped down on to the edge of the bed. My hands trembled as I ripped open the envelope and pulled out the comic book.

The cover showed a close-up of The Masked Mutant. His eyes glared angrily out at the reader. *A NEW FOE FOR THE MUTANT!* proclaimed the title.

Huh? A new foe?

I took a deep breath and held it. Calm down, Skipper, I urged myself. It's only a comic book.

But would this new issue help to solve the mystery for me?

Would it tell me anything about the strange, pink-and-green headquarters building? Would it help solve any of the puzzles from this afternoon?

I turned to the first page. It showed the headquarters building from above. The next drawing showed the building at street level. In the deep shadows, someone was approaching the glass doors.

Someone was sneaking into the headquarters building.

I turned the page.

And shrieked at the top of my lungs: "I don't *believe* it!"

Yes. You probably guessed it. It was *ME* sneaking into The Masked Mutant's headquarters building.

I stared at the page so hard, I thought my eyes were going to pop out of my head.

I was so excited—and so shocked—I couldn't read the words. They became a grey blur.

I turned the pages with shaking hands. I don't think I took a breath. I studied each picture, holding the comic book about an inch from my face.

The Galloping Gazelle sat in a tiny room. The room grew hotter and hotter. In minutes, The Galloping Gazelle would become The Boiled Gazelle!

The Masked Mutant had trapped The Galloping Gazelle in his headquarters. And now he planned to leave The Gazelle there to boil.

I turned the page. My hand shook so hard, I nearly tore the page off.

There I was, creeping through the dark hallway. In the comic, I wore the same T-shirt and baggy jeans I had on right now.

The next drawing showed a close-up of my face. Big balls of sweat rolled down my pink face. I guess that meant I was scared.

I'm a little too chubby in that drawing, I thought.

But it was me. It was definitely ME!

"Mum!" I screamed, closing the comic and jumping off the bed. "Mum! Dad! You have to see this!"

I tore out of my room and hurtled down the stairs. I don't think my feet touched the floor!

"Mum! Dad! Where are you?"

I found them in the kitchen, preparing dinner. Dad was chopping onions by the sink. His eyes were filled with tears. Mum was bent over the stove. As usual, she was having trouble getting the oven lit.

"I'm in this comic book!" I cried, bursting into the room.

"Not now!" they both replied in unison.

"No. You have to see this!" I insisted, waving it in front of Dad.

Dad didn't stop chopping. "You had a letter to the editor published?" he asked through his tears.

"No! I'm *in* the comic!" I told him breathlessly. I waved it closer to him.

"I can't see a thing!" Dad exclaimed. "Get that away from me. Can't you see what this onion is doing to my eyes?"

"There's a trick to chopping onions," Mum said, bent over the stove. "But I don't know what it is."

I ran over to Mum. "You *have* to check this out, Mum. I'm in here. Look. It's really me!"

Mum shook her head, frowning. "I can't get it to light," she said, sighing. "I think the pilot is out again."

"I'll check it if I ever stop crying," Dad told her.

"*Will you look at this?!*" I screamed, totally losing it.

Mum gave a quick glance to the page I was holding in front of her. "Yes, yes. That *does* look a little like you, Skipper," she said, waving me away. She turned back to the oven. "We really need a new stove, dear."

"Dad—take a look," I pleaded.

I ran back to him, but he had shoved a towel up to his face and was crying into the towel. "I guess you can't look now, huh?" I said softly.

He didn't answer. He just cried into the towel.

I let out a long, exasperated moan. What was their problem, anyway?

This was the most exciting thing that had ever happened to me. And they couldn't be bothered to take one look.

71

Angrily, I closed the comic and stomped out of the room.

"Skipper, lay the table," Mum shouted after me.

Lay the table? I'm starring in a famous comic book, and she's asking me to lay the table?

"Why can't Mitzi do it?" I asked.

"Lay the table, Skipper," Mum repeated sternly.

"Okay, okay. In a few minutes," I called back. I dropped down on to the living-room couch and turned to the back of the comic. I had been too excited to read it to the end. Now I wanted to read the part where it tells you what to expect in the next comic book.

My eyes swept over the page. There was The Galloping Gazelle, still trapped in the boiling hot room. And there stood The Masked Mutant outside the door, about to declare his victory.

I squinted at the white thought balloon over The Galloping Gazelle's head. What was he saying?

"Only the boy can save me now," The Galloping Gazelle was thinking. "Only the boy can save the world from The Masked Mutant's evil. But where is he?"

I read it again. And again.

Was it true? Was I the only one who could save The Galloping Gazelle?

Did I really have to go back there?

After school the next day, I hurried to the bus stop. It was a clear, cold day. The ground beneath my trainers was frozen hard. The sky above looked like a broad sheet of cold, blue ice.

Leaning into the sharp wind, I wondered if Libby would be on the bus. I was dying to tell her about the comic book. I wanted to tell her I was going back into the strange building.

Would she go back with me?

No way, I decided. Libby had been frightened after our first visit. I could never drag her back there.

I jogged past the playground, my eyes on the street, watching for a bus.

"Hey, Skipper!" a familiar voice called. I turned to see Wilson running after me, his coat unzipped and flapping up behind him like wings. "Skipper—what's up? You going home?"

Two blocks up, the blue-and-white bus turned the corner.

"No. I'm going somewhere," I told Wilson. "I can't look at your rubber stamp collection now."

His expression turned serious. "I'm not collecting rubber stamps any more," he said. "I've given it up."

I couldn't hide my surprise. "Huh? How come?"

"They took up too much of my time," he replied.

The bus pulled to the kerb. The door opened. "See you later," I told Wilson.

As I stepped on to the bus, I remembered where I was going. And I suddenly wondered if I *would* see Wilson later. I wondered if I would ever see him again!

Libby wasn't on the bus. In a way, I was glad. It meant I wouldn't have to explain to her what I was doing.

She would have laughed at me for believing what I read in a comic book.

But the comic book had told the truth about the Invisibility Curtain. And now it had said that I was the only one who could save The Galloping Gazelle and stop The Masked Mutant's evil.

"But it's just a comic book!" Libby would have said. "How can you be such a jerk to believe a comic book?"

That's what she would have said. And I don't

know *how* I could have answered.

So I was glad she wasn't on the bus.

I climbed off the bus in front of the empty lot. I gazed at it from across the street. I knew it wasn't really an empty lot. I knew the pink-and-green building was there, hidden behind the Invisibility Curtain.

As I crossed the street, I felt a wave of fear sweep down over me. My mouth suddenly got dry. I tried to swallow, but nearly choked. My throat felt as if someone had tied a knot in it. My stomach felt kind of fluttery. And my knees got sweaty and refused to bend.

I stopped on the pavement and struggled to calm myself down.

It's just a comic book. Just a comic book. That's what I told myself, repeating the words over and over.

Finally, staring straight ahead at the empty lot, I worked up my courage enough to move forward. One step. Another. Another.

Suddenly, the building popped into view.

I gasped. Even though I had crossed through the Invisibility Curtain before, it was still amazing to see a building suddenly appear before my eyes.

Swallowing hard, I pulled open one of the glass entrance doors and stepped into the bright, pink-and-yellow lobby.

Staying near the door, I turned to the left, then the right.

Still empty. Not a person in sight.

I coughed. My cough sounded tiny in the huge lobby. My trainers squeaked over the marble floor as I started to the lifts on the far wall.

Where *is* everyone? I asked myself. It's the middle of the afternoon. How can I be the only one in this huge lobby?

I stopped in front of the lifts. I raised my finger to the lift button—but I didn't push it.

I wish Libby *had* come along, I decided. If Libby were here, at least I'd have someone to be terrified *with*!

I pushed the lift button.

"Well . . . here goes," I murmured, waiting for the door to open.

And then someone laughed. A cold, evil laugh.

Right behind me.

I let out a low cry and spun around.

No one there.

The laughter repeated. Soft, but cruel.

My eyes darted around the lobby. I couldn't see anyone.

"Wh-who's there?" I choked out.

The laughter stopped.

I continued to search. My eyes went up to the wall above the lift. A small, black loudspeaker poked out from the yellow wall.

The laughter must have come from there, I decided. I stared up at it as if I expected to see someone in there.

Get out of here! a voice inside me begged. My sensible voice. *Just turn around, Skipper, and run out of this building as fast as your rubbery, shaky legs will take you!*

I ignored it and pressed the lift button. The lift door on the left slid open silently, and I stepped inside.

The door closed. I stared at the control panel. Should I push up or down?

The last visit, I had pushed up, the top floor— and the lift had taken Libby and me down to the basement.

My finger hesitated in front of the buttons. What would happen if this time I pushed *down*?

I didn't get a chance to find out. The lift started with a jolt before I pushed any button at all.

I grabbed on to the railing. My hand was cold and wet. The lift hummed as it rose.

I'm going up, I realized. Up to where?

The ride seemed to take for ever. I watched the floor numbers whir by on top of the control panel. Forty ... forty-one ... forty-two ... The lift beeped each time it passed a floor.

It came to a stop at forty-six. Was this the top floor?

The door slid open. I let go of the railing and stepped out.

I glanced down a long, grey hallway. I blinked once. Twice. It looked as if I had stepped into a black-and-white movie. The walls were grey. The ceiling was grey. The floor was grey. The doors on both sides of the hall were grey.

It feels like I'm standing in a thick, grey fog, I thought, peering one way, then the other. Or in a dark cloud.

No one in sight. Nothing moving.

I listened hard. Listened for voices, for laughter, for the click and hum of office machinery.

Silence—except for the thudding of my heart.

I shoved my cold, clammy hands into the pockets of my jeans and began to walk, slowly following the hallway.

I turned a corner and stared down another endless, grey hallway. The end of the hall seemed to fade away, to fade into a grey blur.

I suddenly remembered the drawings in the newest issue of *The Masked Mutant*. A big, two-page drawing had shown the long hallways of The Masked Mutant's secret headquarters.

The long, twisting hallway in the comic book looked just like this hallway—except that the comic book hallway had bright green walls and a yellow ceiling. And the rooms were filled with costumed supervillains who worked for The Masked Mutant.

As I slowly made my way through this grey, empty hallway, I had a weird thought. Everything looked so grey and washed out, I had the feeling that I was in a sketch of a hallway. A black-and-white pencil drawing that hadn't been filled in yet.

But, of course, that didn't make any sense at all.

You're just thinking crazy thoughts because you're so scared, I told myself.

And then I heard a noise.

A hard, thumping sound. A bump.

"Whoa!" I whispered. My heart leaped up to my throat. I stopped in the middle of the hall. And listened.

Bump. Thump.

Coming from up ahead. From around the next corner?

I forced myself to walk. I turned the corner. And gasped at the bright colours.

The walls down *this* hallway were bright green. The ceiling was yellow. The thick carpet under my sneakers was a dark, wine-red.

Bump. Bump. Thump.

The colours were so bright, I had to shield my eyes with one hand.

I squinted to the end of the hall. The green walls led to a closed yellow door. The door had a metal bolt against the front.

Thump. Thump.

The sounds were coming from behind the bolted doorway.

I made my way slowly down the hall to the doorway.

I stopped outside the bolted door. "Anyone in there?" I tried to call into the room. But my voice came out in a choked whisper.

I coughed and tried again. "Anyone in there?"

No reply.

Then, another loud bumping sound. Like wood thumping against wood.

"Anyone in there?" I called, my voice a little stronger.

The thumping sounds stopped. "Can you help me?" a man's voice called from inside the room.

I froze.

"Can you help me?" the man pleaded.

I hesitated for a second. Should I try to help him?

Yes.

I raised both hands to the metal bolt. I took a deep breath and shoved the bolt with all my strength.

To my surprise, it slid easily.

The door was unlocked. I turned the handle and pushed the door open.

I stumbled off-balance into the room and stared in amazement at the figure staring back at me.

"You—you're *real*?" I cried.

His cape was twisted, and his mask had rolled down over one eye. But I knew I was staring at The Galloping Gazelle.

"You're really *alive*?" I blurted out.

"Of course," he replied impatiently. "Untie me, kid." He gazed towards the open door. "You'd better hurry."

I realized that his powerful arms and legs were tied to the chair. The thumping and bumping had been the sounds of his chair banging against the floor as he tried to escape.

"I—I can't believe that you're here!" I cried. I was so amazed—and so frightened—I didn't know what I was saying!

"I'll give you my autograph later," he said, his eyes still on the doorway. "Just hurry, okay? We've got to get out of here. I don't think we have much time."

"T-time?" I stammered.

"He'll be back," The Galloping Gazelle

murmured. "We want to get to him before he gets to *us*, right, kid?"

"Us??" I cried.

"Just untie me," The Galloping Gazelle instructed. "I can handle him." He shook his head. "I wish I could contact my buddies at the League. They're probably all searching the universe for me."

Still half dazed, I stumbled across the tiny room to the chair and began working at the ropes. The knots were big and tight and hard to untie. The coarse rope scraped my hands as I struggled to loosen them.

"Hurry, kid," The Galloping Gazelle urged. "Hey, how did you find the secret headquarters, anyway?"

"I . . . just found it," I replied, tugging at the knots.

"Don't be modest, kid," the superhero said in his flat, low voice. "You used your secret cyber-radar powers, right? Or did you use ultra-mind control to read my thoughts and hurry to my rescue?"

"No. I just took the bus," I replied.

I didn't really know how to answer him. Did he have me confused with someone else?

Why was I here? What was going to happen to us? To *me*?

Questions, questions. They flew through my mind as I frantically worked at the heavy ropes.

I tried to ignore the pain from the cuts and scrapes to my hands. But it hurt a lot.

Finally, one of the knots slid open. The Galloping Gazelle flexed his muscles and stretched out his powerful chest—and the ropes popped away easily.

"Thanks, kid," he boomed, jumping to his feet. He adjusted his mask so that he could see through both eyeholes. Then he swept his long cape behind him and straightened his tights.

"Okay. Let's go pay him a surprise visit," he said, pulling up the ends of his gloves. He started towards the door, taking long, heavy strides. His boots thundered loudly as he walked.

"Uh . . . do you really want *me* to come, too?" I asked, lingering behind the chair.

He nodded. "I know what you're worried about, kid. You're worried that you won't be able to keep up with me because I have dyno-legs and I'm the fastest living mutant in the known universe."

"Well . . ." I hesitated.

"Don't worry," he replied. "I'll go slow." He motioned impatiently. "Let's get moving."

I tripped over the tangle of ropes on the floor. Grabbed the chair to catch my balance. Then followed him out into the green-and-yellow hallway.

He turned and began running down the hall.

As I started to follow, he became a blue-and-red blur of light—and then vanished.

A few seconds later, he came jogging back. "Sorry. Too fast for you?" he called.

I nodded. "A little."

He rested a gloved hand heavily on my shoulder. His grey eyes peered at me solemnly through the slits in his mask. "Do you have wall-climbing abilities?" he demanded.

I shook my head. "No. Sorry."

"Okay. We'll take the stairs," he said.

He grabbed my hand and pulled me down the hall. He moved so fast, both of my feet were in the air.

I guess it was impossible for him to go slow.

The walls whirred past in a bright green blur. He pulled me around a corner, then another corner.

I felt as if I were flying! We were moving so fast, I didn't have time to breathe.

Around another corner. Then through an open doorway.

The doorway led to a flight of steep, dark stairs. I peered up to the top, but I could see only heavy blackness.

I expected The Galloping Gazelle to pull me up the stairs. But to my surprise, he stopped just past the doorway.

He narrowed his eyes at the stairs. "There is a

85

disintegrator-ray there," he announced, rubbing his square jaw thoughtfully.

"A *what*?" I cried.

"A disintegrator-ray," he repeated, his eyes locked on the stairs. "If you step into it, it will disintegrate you in one hundredth of a second."

I swallowed hard. My entire body started to tremble.

"Do you think you can jump the first two steps?" The Galloping Gazelle asked.

"You mean—?" I started.

"Land on the third step," he instructed. "Get a good running start."

I'll need it, I thought, staring at the steep steps.

I suddenly wished I hadn't eaten so many Pop-Tarts and bowls of Frosted Flakes for breakfast every morning. If only I were a little slimmer, a little lighter.

"Get a good running start and make sure you clear the first two steps," The Galloping Gazelle warned. "Land on the third step and keep moving. If you land on the first or second step, you'll disintegrate." He motioned with his fingers. "Poof."

I let out a low, frightened moan. I couldn't help myself. I wanted to be brave. But my body wasn't cooperating. It was shaking and quaking as if I were made of jelly.

"I'll go first," the superhero said. He turned to

the stairs, bent his knees, stretched both hands forward—and leaped over the invisible disintegrator-ray. He landed on the fifth step.

He turned around and motioned for me to follow. "See? It's easy," he said brightly.

Easy for you! I thought darkly. *Some of us don't have dyno-legs.*

"Hurry," he urged. "If you stop to think about it, you won't be able to do it."

I'm *already* thinking about it! I thought.

How can I *not* think about it?

"I—I'm not very athletic," I murmured in a tiny, trembling voice. What an understatement! Whenever the kids I know play any sports, I am always the *last* kid chosen for a team.

"Hurry," The Galloping Gazelle urged. He reached out both hands. "Take a good running jump, kid. Aim for the third step. It isn't that high. I'll catch you."

The third step looked about a mile in the air to me. But I held my breath, bent my knees, took a running leap—my *best* leap—

—and I landed with a hard *thud* on the first step.

I screamed and clamped my eyes shut as the disintegrator-ray poured through me, and my body crumbled into thin air.

Actually, I didn't feel anything.

I opened my eyes to find myself still standing on the bottom step. Still in one chubby piece.

"I—I—I—" I stammered.

"I guess he doesn't have it turned on," The Galloping Gazelle said calmly. He smiled at me through the mask. "You had a lucky escape, kid."

I was still trembling. Cold beads of sweat rolled down my forehead. I couldn't speak.

"Hope your luck holds out," The Galloping Gazelle muttered. He turned and started up the stairs, his cape floating behind him. "Come on. Let's go meet our destiny."

I didn't like the sound of that. Not one bit.

But I didn't like anything that was going on. The Galloping Gazelle had said that I was lucky.

But I certainly didn't feel lucky as I followed him up the dark stairs.

At the top landing, he pushed open a wide metal door, and we stepped into an amazing room.

The room glowed with colour. It was decorated like an office, the fanciest, most luxurious office I have ever seen.

The shaggy white carpet was soft and so thick, I sank in it nearly to my ankles. Silky blue curtains were draped over enormous windows that overlooked the town. Sparkly crystal chandeliers hung from the ceiling.

Velvety couches and chairs were arranged around dark wood tables. One wall was covered with floor-to-ceiling bookshelves, each shelf filled with leather-covered books.

A giant TV screen—dark—stood in one corner. Beside it, a wall of electronic equipment. Enormous oil paintings of green farm fields covered one wall.

A shiny, gold-plated desk stood in the middle of the room. The tall desk chair behind it looked more like a throne than a chair.

"Wow!" I cried, lingering near the door, my eyes taking in the splendour of the vast room.

"He treats himself well," The Galloping Gazelle commented. "But his time is over."

"You mean—?" I started.

"I'm too fast for him," the superhero boasted.

"I'll run circles around him, faster and faster—until I become a raging tornado. He'll be swept away for ever."

"Wow," I repeated. I didn't know what else to say.

"He caught me napping before," The Galloping Gazelle continued. "That's the only way he can catch me. When I'm asleep. Otherwise, I'm much too fast for him. Too fast for anybody. Know how fast I run the one-hundred metres?"

"How fast?" I asked.

"I run it in one-tenth. One-tenth of a second. That would be an Olympic record. But they don't let me in the Olympics because I'm a mutant."

I started to follow The Galloping Gazelle to the centre of the room. But I stopped when I heard the laughter.

The same cold laughter I had heard in the lobby.

I froze in fright.

And stared as the gold desk began to move. And change.

The shiny gold shimmered as it shifted and bent, raising itself up and forming a human figure.

I took a step back, trying to hide behind The Galloping Gazelle as the desk melted away—and The Masked Mutant rose up in its place.

His dark eyes burned menacingly through the slits in his mask. He was a lot taller than he appeared in the comic. And a lot more powerful-looking.

And a lot scarier.

He raised a fist at The Galloping Gazelle. "You dare to invade my private office?" he demanded.

"Say goodbye to all this ill-gotten splendour," The Galloping Gazelle told the Mutant.

"I'll say goodbye to *you*!" The Masked Mutant shot back, spitting the words angrily.

Then he turned his frightening, cold eyes on me. "I'll handle you easily, Gazelle," the world's most evil supervillain said softly. "But, *first*, watch me destroy the kid!"

I shrank back as The Masked Mutant took a step towards me, his fist still raised, his black eyes glaring furiously into mine.

My heart pounding, I turned and frantically searched for a hiding place.

But there was nowhere to hide.

And I couldn't make a run for it. The door slammed shut as The Masked Mutant moved closer.

"Whoa!" I cried. I raised both hands in front of my face, as if shielding myself.

I couldn't bear to see his cold, cruel eyes glaring at me as he approached.

He's going to *destroy* me, I thought. But I don't have to watch!

And, then, as The Masked Mutant took one more step, The Galloping Gazelle moved to block his way. "You'll deal with *me*, Mutant!" he declared in his booming voice. "If you want the kid, you'll have to take me out first."

"No problem," The Masked Mutant declared softly.

But his expression changed as The Galloping Gazelle began to circle him. Faster and faster—until the Gazelle appeared to disappear into a whirling, spinning tornado of blue and red.

The Gazelle is carrying out his plan, I realized as I backed up to the wall. He's going to run faster and faster around The Masked Mutant until he creates a whirlwind that will blow the evil Mutant away.

Pressing my back against the wall, I watched the amazing battle eagerly. The Galloping Gazelle whirled faster. Faster. So fast, a powerful wind swept over the room, slapping the curtains, toppling over a vase of flowers, sending books flying from the shelves.

Yes! I thought happily, shooting both fists into the air. *Yes!* We win! We win!

I lowered my hands and let out a horrified groan when I saw The Masked Mutant casually stick his foot out.

The Galloping Gazelle tripped over the foot and slammed face down on to the floor with a shattering *thud.*

He bounced hard a couple of times and then lay still.

The wind stopped. The curtains fell back in place.

The Masked Mutant stood over the fallen

superhero, hands triumphantly on the waist of his costume.

"Get up!" I screamed, without even realizing I was doing it. "Get up, Gazelle! Please!"

The Gazelle groaned, but didn't move.

"Dinnertime," sneered The Masked Mutant.

My back pressed hard against the wall, I stared in horror as The Mutant began to change again. His face twisted and appeared to flatten. His body lowered, and he leaned forward, spreading his hands on the floor.

He stepped forward as a snarling leopard. Tilting its head to one side, the leopard uttered a ferocious growl of attack.

Then it arched its back, tensed its back legs— and leaped on to the sprawled body of The Galloping Gazelle.

"Get up! Get up, Gazelle!" I shrieked as the leopard attacked.

The Masked Mutant clawed and gnawed at the helpless Gazelle.

"Get up! Get *up*!" I screamed.

To my shock, The Galloping Gazelle opened his eyes.

The ferocious leopard ripped away the bottom of The Gazelle's mask with its teeth.

The Galloping Gazelle rolled out from under the enormous beast and scrambled to his feet.

With a roar, the leopard swiped its paws,

sending a long tear down the length of The Gazelle's cape.

"I'm *outta* here!" The Gazelle cried, making tracks to the door. He turned back to me. "You're on your own, kid!"

"No! Wait!" I screamed.

I don't think The Gazelle heard me. He shoved open the door with one shoulder and vanished.

The door slammed behind him.

Quickly, the leopard changed, rising up on its hind legs, its body shifting and moving—until The Masked Mutant stepped forward.

He smiled at me as he approached, a cold, menacing smile.

"You're on your own, kid," he said softly.

I edged along the wall as The Masked Mutant moved slowly, steadily towards me. I knew I couldn't get to the door, as The Galloping Gazelle had. I wasn't fast enough.

He should call himself The Galloping *Chicken*! I thought bitterly.

How could he save his own skin and leave me here like this?

I couldn't run. I couldn't fight. What could I do?

What could I do against a deadly foe who could turn himself into anything solid?

The Masked Mutant stopped in the centre of the room, hands on his waist, his dark eyes twinkling. He was enjoying my fright. And already tasting his victory.

"What are your powers, kid?" he demanded, a sneer in his voice.

"Huh?" His question caught me by surprise.

"What are your powers?" he repeated

impatiently, swirling his cape behind him. "Do you shrink down to a tiny bug? Is that your secret?"

"Huh? Shrink? Me?" I was shaking so hard, I couldn't think straight.

Why was he asking me these questions?

"Do you burst into flames?" he continued, moving closer. "Is that your power? Are you magnetic? Are you a mind-fogger?" His voice turned angry. "What *is* it? *Answer* me! What is your power?"

"I—I don't have any powers," I stammered. If I pressed any harder into the wall, I'd become part of the wallpaper!

The Masked Mutant laughed. "So you won't tell me, huh? Okay, okay. Have it your way."

His smile faded. His dark eyes turned cold and hard. "I was just trying to make it easy on you," he said, moving even closer. "I want to destroy you in the easiest way possible."

"Oh. I see," I muttered.

My eye caught something on the shelf. A large, smooth stone as big as a coconut. It was some kind of decoration. I wondered if it would make a good weapon.

"Say bye-bye, kid," he said through clenched teeth.

He came towards me quickly.

And as he moved, I grabbed the big stone off the shelf. It was a lot heavier than I'd thought. It wasn't stone, I realized. It was shaped like a smooth stone. But it was made of solid steel.

I hoisted it up and took careful aim. Then I heaved it at The Masked Mutant's head.

And missed.

The stone thudded heavily on to the carpet.

"Nice try," he muttered . . .

. . . and moved quickly to destroy me.

I tried to duck away from him, but he was too quick.

His powerful hands grabbed me around the waist and lifted me off the floor.

Higher. Higher.

I realized he was moving his molecules, making his arms stretch until he had lifted me above the chandelier.

I thrashed my arms and legs and tried to squirm away. But he was too strong.

Higher. Higher. Until my head banged hard against the ceiling, at least twenty feet above the floor.

"Happy landings!" The Masked Mutant cried gleefully as he prepared to drop me and send me plummeting to my doom.

But before he could drop me, I heard the door swing open.

The Masked Mutant heard it, too. Holding me suspended in the air, he turned to see who had entered. "You!" he cried in surprise.

High above the floor, I squirmed around and bent my head to see through the chandelier. The light sparkled through the crystals, making it impossible to see.

"How dare you burst in here!" The Masked Mutant cried to the intruder.

He lowered me a little. Just enough for me to see the doorway.

"Libby!" I cried. "What are *you* doing here?"

The Masked Mutant lowered me to the floor and turned to face Libby. My legs were wobbling so badly, I had to grab on to a bookshelf to hold myself up.

"Libby—get *out* of here! Get away!" I tried to warn her.

But she stormed into the room, her red hair flying behind her. She had her eyes on me and completely ignored The Masked Mutant.

Doesn't she *know* that he is the most evil supervillain in the known universe?

"Skipper—didn't you hear me calling you?" Libby demanded sharply.

"Huh? Libby—"

"I was across the street," she said. "I saw you going into this building. I called to you."

"I—I didn't hear you," I stammered. "Listen, you'd better get *out* of here, Libby."

"I've been searching and searching for you," she continued, ignoring my warning, ignoring my frantic gestures. "What are you *doing* in here, Skipper?"

"Uh ... I really can't talk right now," I replied, pointing to The Masked Mutant.

He stood impatiently, hands at his waist, tapping his boot on the carpet. "I see that I will have to destroy you both," he said quietly.

Libby spun around. She seemed to notice the supervillain for the first time. "Skipper and I are leaving now," she said with a sneer.

I gasped. *Didn't she know who she was talking to?*

No. Of course she didn't know. She reads only *High School Harry & Beanhead* comics. She has no idea how much danger we are in! I realized.

"I'm sorry," The Masked Mutant replied, sneering back at Libby from under his mask. "You are not leaving. In fact, you are never leaving this building again."

Libby glared back at him, and I saw her expression change. Her green eyes grew wide, and her mouth dropped open.

She took a step back until she stood beside me. "We have to do something," she whispered.

Do something?

What could *we* do against the monstrous mega-mutant?

I swallowed hard. I couldn't think of how to answer her.

The Masked Mutant tossed back his cape and

took a step towards us. "Which one of you wants to go first?" he demanded softly.

I turned and saw that Libby had backed up to the bookshelves. She pulled a yellow plastic toy gun from her backpack.

"Libby—what are you *doing*?" I whispered. "That's just a toy!"

"I know," she whispered back. "But this is a comic book—right? It can't be real. So if it's a comic book, we can do *anything*!"

She raised the plastic toy pistol and aimed it at The Masked Mutant.

He let out a cold laugh. "What do you plan to do with that toy?" he asked scornfully.

"It only l-looks like a toy," Libby stammered. "It's a Molecule-Melter. Leave this room—or I'll melt all your molecules!"

The Mutant's smile grew wider. "Nice try," he said, flashing two rows of perfect, white teeth.

He narrowed his eyes at Libby and took another step towards her. "I guess you want to go first. I'll try not to hurt you—too much."

Libby held the toy gun in front of her with both hands. She gritted her teeth, preparing to pull the trigger.

"Put down that toy. It can't help you," The Masked Mutant declared, moving closer.

"I'm not kidding," Libby insisted in a shrill voice. "It isn't a toy. It really *is* a Molecule-Melter."

The Masked Mutant laughed again and took another step closer. Then another step.

Libby aimed the gun at The Mutant's chest. She pulled the trigger.

A high-pitched whistle burst out of the gun.

The Masked Mutant took another step closer. Then another.

Libby lowered the plastic gun.

We both stared in horror as The Masked Mutant came nearer.

He took one more step. Then stopped.

A bright white light circled his body. The light became a crackling electrical current.

The Mutant uttered a low moan. Then he began to melt.

His head melted down into his mask. Tinier and tinier—until it disappeared completely. The empty mask slumped on to the shoulders of his costume. And then the rest of his body melted away, shrinking until there was nothing left but a wrinkled costume and cape, heaped on the carpet.

Libby and I stood staring down at the costume in silence.

"It—it worked!" I finally managed to choke out. "The toy gun—it worked, Libby!"

"Of course," she replied with surprising calm.

She walked over to the empty costume and kicked it with her trainer. "Of course it worked. I warned him it was a Molecule-Melter. He wouldn't listen."

My brain was doing flip-flops. I didn't really understand. It was just a toy pistol. Why did it destroy the mightiest mutant on Earth?

"Let's get out of here!" I pleaded, starting towards the door.

Libby moved to block my path. "I'm sorry, Skipper," she said softly.

"Sorry? What do you mean?"

She raised the plastic pistol and aimed it at me. "I'm sorry," she said, "because you're disappearing next."

At first I thought Libby was joking. "Libby, put down the gun," I told her. "You have a *sick* sense of humour!"

She kept the plastic gun aimed at my chest.

I let out a feeble laugh.

But I quickly cut it short when I saw the hard expression on her face. "Libby—what's your problem?" I demanded.

"I'm not Libby," she replied softly. "I hate to break the news to you, Skipper—but there *is* no Libby."

As she said those words, she began to change. Her red hair slid into her head. Her cheeks grew wider. Her nose lengthened. Her eyes changed from green to black.

She stretched up, growing taller. Muscles bulged on her skinny arms. And as she grew, her clothing changed, too. Her jeans and T-shirt appeared to melt away—replaced by a familiar-looking costume.

107

The costume of The Masked Mutant.

"Libby—what's going on?" I cried in a tiny, frightened voice. I still didn't understand. "How are you doing that?"

She shook her head. "You don't catch on very fast, do you?" she said, rolling her eyes. Her voice came out deep and booming. A man's voice.

"Libby, I—"

She swept her cape behind her. "I'm The Masked Mutant, Skipper. I changed my molecules into a girl your age and called myself Libby. But I'm The Masked Mutant."

"But—but—but—" I sputtered.

She tossed the toy gun aside and grinned at me triumphantly.

"But you just *melted* The Masked Mutant!" I cried. "We both saw him melt!"

She shook her head. "No. You're mistaken. I just melted The Magnificent Molecule Man."

I gaped at her in astonishment. "Huh? Molecule Man?"

"He worked for me," she explained, glancing down at the crumpled, empty costume on the floor. "Sometimes I ordered him to dress like me. To keep people off my track."

"He worked for you—and you *melted* him?" I cried.

"I'm a villain," The Masked Mutant replied, smiling. "I do very bad things—remember?"

It all started to come clear. There never was a Libby. It had been The Masked Mutant all along.

The Masked Mutant stepped over the crumpled costume to move closer to me. Once again, I pressed my back against the wall. "Now I have no choice. Now I have to do something very bad to you, Skipper," he said flatly, his black eyes staring hard into mine through his mask.

"But—why?" I cried. "Why can't I just leave? I'll go straight home. I'll never tell anyone about you. Really!" I pleaded.

He shook his head. "I can't let you leave. You belong here now."

"Huh?" I gasped. "What are you *saying*, Libby—I mean, Mutant?"

"You belong here now, Skipper," he replied coldly. "I knew it when I saw you on the bus for the first time. I knew you were perfect when you told me you knew *everything* about my comics."

"But—but—" I sputtered again.

"It's so hard to find good characters for my stories, Skipper. It's so hard to find good foes. I'm always looking for new faces. That's why I was so pleased when I discovered you."

His evil grin grew wider. "Then when you recognized my headquarters building, I knew you were right. I knew you were ready to star in a story."

The smile faded quickly. "I'm so sorry, Skipper. But the story is over. Your part has come to an end."

"What—what are you going to do?" I stammered.

"Destroy you, of course!" The Mutant replied coldly.

I pressed my back against the wall. I stared back at him, thinking hard.

"Goodbye, Skipper," The Masked Mutant said softly.

"But you can't do this!" I screamed. "You're just a character in a comic book! But I'm real! I'm a real, live person! I'm a real boy!"

A strange smile formed on The Mutant's lips. "No, you're not, Skipper," he said, sniggering. "You're not real. You're just like me now. You're a comic book character, too."

I pinched my arm. It felt as warm and real as always.

"You're a liar!" I shouted.

The Masked Mutant nodded. A pleased smile formed on his face. "Yes, I'm a liar," he agreed. "That's one of my *better* qualities." His smile faded. "But I'm not lying this time, Skipper. You're not real any more."

I refused to believe him. "I feel the way I always have," I declared.

"But I changed you into a comic book character," he insisted. "Remember when you entered this building for the first time? Remember when you walked through the glass door and a beam of light passed over you?"

I nodded. "Yes. I remember that," I muttered.

"Well, that was a scanner," The Masked Mutant continued. "When you stepped through it, it scanned your body. It turned you into tiny dots of ink."

"No!" I shouted.

He ignored my cry. "That's all you are now, Skipper. Tiny dots of red, blue, and yellow ink. You're a comic book character, just like me."

He slid towards me menacingly, his cape spreading out behind him. "But I'm sorry to say you've made your last appearance in my comic book. Or in *any* comic book."

"Wait!" I cried.

"I can't wait any longer," The Masked Mutant replied coldly. "I've already wasted too much time on you, Skipper."

"But I'm not Skipper!" I declared.

"I'm not Skipper Matthews," I said. "There *is* no Skipper Matthews."

"Oh, really?" he asked, rolling his eyes. "Then who are you?"

"I'm The Colossal Elastic Boy!" I replied.

The Masked Mutant uttered a low gasp. "Elastic Boy!" he exclaimed. "I *thought* you looked familiar!"

"Goodbye, Mutant," I said in a deep voice.

"Where are you going?" he asked sharply.

"Back to my home planet of Xargos," I replied, starting towards the door. "I'm not allowed to guest-star in other comic books."

He moved quickly to block the door. "Nice try, Elastic Boy," he said. "But you have invaded my secret headquarters. I have to destroy you."

I laughed. "You can't destroy Elastic Boy!" I boasted. "I'll stretch out my elastic arms and wrap you in them, and squeeze you into Play-Doh!"

"I don't think so," The Masked Mutant replied dryly. He let out an angry growl. "I'm tired of all this talk, talk, talk. I'm going to tear you to pieces—and then tear your pieces into tiny pieces!"

I laughed again. "No way!" I told him. "I'm elastic, remember? I *can't* be torn into pieces. I bend—but I don't break! There's only one way that Elastic Boy can be destroyed!"

"What's that?" The Masked Mutant asked.

"By sulphuric acid," I replied. "That's the only thing that can destroy my elastic body!"

A pleased smile spread behind the masked face.

"Oops!" I cried. "I didn't mean to let that slip out!"

I tried to make it to the door. But I wasn't fast enough.

I saw The Masked Mutant quickly begin to change. He changed into a steaming hot wave of sulphuric acid.

And before I could move, the tall wave of acid swept towards me.

With a loud cry, I leaped away.

The tall wave swept past. It missed me by inches.

I turned and watched it splash over the carpet. The carpet began to sizzle and burn.

"Yes!" I shouted gleefully. "Yes!"

I had never felt so happy, so strong, so triumphant!

I had defeated The Masked Mutant. I had totally tricked him. I had destroyed the most evil supervillain ever to walk the planet!

Me! A twelve-year-old boy named Skipper Matthews! I had sent The Masked Mutant to his doom!

Such a simple trick. But it had worked.

From reading the comics, I knew that The Masked Mutant could change his molecules into anything solid. And then change back again.

But I tricked him into changing himself into a

liquid! And once he changed into a liquid, he could not re-form himself.

The Masked Mutant was gone for ever.

"Skipper, you are a clever guy!" I shouted out loud. I was so happy, I did a little dance on the thick carpet.

I couldn't *believe* The Masked Mutant had believed that I was Elastic Boy. I'd made that name up. I've never *heard* of any Elastic Boy!

But he fell for it. And now the evil supervillain is gone! I thought happily.

And I am alive! Alive!

I couldn't wait to get home and see my family again. The bus ride seemed to take hours.

Finally, I was running up my front lawn. Into the house through the front door.

I immediately saw a brown envelope lying on the mail table. The new issue of *The Masked Mutant*.

Who needs it? I asked myself.

I ignored it and hurried to say hi to my parents. I was so glad to be home, I was even happy to see Mitzi. "Mitzi—how about a game of Frisbee?" I asked.

"Huh?" She gaped at me in shock. I never want to play anything with my little sister.

But, today, I just wanted to be happy and celebrate being alive.

Mitzi and I hurried out to the back garden. We

threw a Frisbee around for about half an hour. We had a great time.

"How about a snack?" I asked her.

"Yeah, I'm starving," she replied. "Mum left some chocolate cake on the counter."

Chocolate cake sounded just right.

Humming happily to myself, I trotted into the kitchen. I pulled down two plates from the cabinet. Then I found the big cake knife in the drawer.

"Don't make your slice bigger than mine!" Mitzi warned, watching me carefully as I prepared to cut the cake.

"Mitzi, I promise I won't cheat you," I said sweetly. I was in such a good mood, even Mitzi couldn't get me upset.

"This looks like awesome chocolate cake!" I exclaimed.

I slid the big knife over the cake.

It slipped.

"Ow!" I cried out as the knife blade cut the back of my hand.

I raised my hand and stared down at the cut. "Hey!" I uttered in surprise.

What was trickling out from the cut?

Not blood.

It was red, blue, yellow, and black.

INK!

"Cool!" Mitzi cried.

"Where's that new *Masked Mutant* comic?" I asked. I suddenly had the feeling that my comic book career wasn't over!

Add *more*

Goosebumps

to your collection . . .
A chilling preview of
what's next from
R.L. Stine

My Hairiest Adventure

Why were there so many stray dogs in my town?

And why did they always choose *me* to chase?

Did they wait quietly in the woods, watching people go by? Then did they whisper to each other, "See that blond kid? That's Larry Boyd—let's go get him!"?

I ran as fast as I could. But it's hard to run when you're carrying a guitar case. It kept banging against my leg.

And I kept slipping in the snow.

The dogs were catching up. They were howling and barking, trying to scare me to death.

Well, it's working, guys! I thought. I'm scared. I'm plenty scared!

Dogs are supposed to sense when you're afraid of them. But I'm not usually afraid of dogs. In fact, I really like dogs.

I'm only afraid of dogs when there's a pack of them, running furiously after me, drooling hungrily, eager to tear me to tiny shreds. Like now.

Scrambling over the snow, I nearly toppled into a drift up to my knees. I glanced back. The dogs were gaining on me.

It isn't fair! I thought bitterly. They have four legs, and I only have two!

The big, black dog with the evil, black eyes was leading the pack, as usual. He had his lips pulled back in an angry snarl. He was close enough so that I could see his sharp, pointy teeth.

"Go home! Go home! Bad dogs! Go home!"

Why was I yelling at them? They didn't even *have* homes!

"Go home! Go home!"

My boots slipped in the snow, and the weight of my guitar case nearly pulled me over. Somehow I staggered forward, caught my balance, and kept moving.

My heart was pounding like crazy. And I felt as if I were burning up, even though it was about twelve degrees.

I squinted against the bright glare of the snow. I struggled to run faster, but my leg muscles were starting to cramp.

I don't stand a chance! I realized.

"Ow!" The heavy guitar case bounced against my side.

I glanced back. The dogs were leaping

excitedly, making wide criss-crosses across the yards, howling and yowling, as they scrambled after me.

Moving closer. And closer.

"Go home! Bad dogs! Bad! Go home!"

Why me?

I'm a nice guy. Really. Ask anybody. They'll tell you—Larry Boyd is the nicest twelve-year-old kid in town!

So why did they always chase *me*?

The last time, I dived into a parked car and shut the door just as they pounced. But today, the dogs were too close. And the cars along the street were all snow-covered. By the time I got a car door open, the dogs would be having me for dessert!

I was only half a block from Lily's house. I could see it on the corner across the street. It was my only chance.

If I could get to Lily's house, I could—

"NOOOOOOOO!"

I slipped on a small rock, hidden under the snow. The guitar case flew from my hand and hit the snow with a soft *thud*.

I was down. Face down in the snow.

"They've got me this time," I moaned. "They've got me."